Nellie McClung

Mary Lile Benham

Fitzhenry & Whiteside Limited

Contents

THE CANADIANS
A Continuing Series

Nellie McClung

Author: Mary Lile Benham
Design: Kerry Designs
Cover Illustration: John Mardon

Fitzhenry & Whiteside acknowledge with thanks the support of the Government of Canada through its Book Publishing Industry Development Program.

Canadian Cataloguing in Publication Data
Benham, Mary Lile
Nellie McClung
(The Canadians)
Rev. ed.
Includes bibliographical references and index.
ISBN 1-55041-477-9
1. McClung, Nellie, 1873-1951. 2. Feminists – Canada – Biography – Juvenile literature. I. Title. II. Series
FC521.M3W32 1999   971.05'1'092   C99-932550-7

© 2000 Fitzhenry & Whiteside Limited
195 Allstate Parkway, Markham, Ontario L3R 4T8

Prologue
Privy Council Declares that Women Are Persons

That was the headline in 1929. It was that declaration which made it possible for women to be appointed to the Canadian Senate. The efforts of years of female agitation were finally rewarded. And the dynamo behind it all was Nellie McClung, the Holy Terror, the Hyena in Petticoats, the latter-day Joan of Arc leading her battalions of women against the bastions of political power, using words as weapons.

She was spirited, she was amusing, she was effective. Her voice was liltingly Irish, and she was attractive in all her roles – as wife, mother, ardent advocate of women's rights, midwife at the birth of women's suffrage (the right to vote), teacher, lecturer, legislator and writer. She was threatened with violence and libel suits. She was burned in effigy. But she was "our Nell" to a cast of thousands.

A petite, pretty, sparkling-eyed westerner with deep Christian convictions and a devotion to the significance of family life, Nellie McClung throughout her long, diverse career was to be a potent influence on Canadian society.

Lord Chancellor Sankey at Temple Bar, 1929, on his way to deliver the judgment that women are "persons"

Chapter 1
Looking Westward

"A doctor is alright in the case of a broken arm or maybe scarlet fever, but an increase in the population is a natural thing surely," sniffed one of the neighbours who had come in to lend a hand. They were all offended that John Mooney had arranged for a doctor to officiate at the birth of his sixth child, Helen Letitia, on October 20th, 1873. One lusty yell announced to the world that "Windy Nellie," with her tongue hung in the middle and wagging at both ends, had arrived.

The birth took place in the Mooney farmhouse at Chatsworth in Grey County, Ontario. One hundred acres of land belonged to the farmhouse: a fifty-acre free grant, plus another fifty acres which John had earned by logging. He had learned his logging skills in Bytown (Ottawa), where, at eighteen, he had first arrived in Canada after a ten-week sea-voyage from Ireland.

John Mooney had married Letitia McCurdy from Dundee, Scotland, in 1858 and brought her to this farmhouse, with its well-scrubbed, pine-board floor, and its interior decoration of dried apples and smoked hams hanging in brown festoons from the rafters. The world-wide agricultural depression of the 1870s meant rough years for farmers. Nellie was born into a household where, if a child needed a copybook and a pen, he or she had to sell a basket of eggs to pay the shot.

Every member of the family had to toil to claw a living from the stony soil of Grey County. Letitia Mooney yearned for better opportunities for her two sons. When men returned to Grey County with tales of a land where "the strawberries are so plentiful and luscious that the oxen's feet are red with them as they plow the willing sod," she was determined that her family too would look westward to this land of promise.

The family was further encouraged to move west by the Dominion Lands Act of 1872, under the terms of which a settler was given (after payment of a $10 office fee) a homestead of a quarter section of land (160 acres), subject to at least six months' residence and cultivation of the land each year for three years.

The oldest son, Will, an ambitious and adventurous young man, went west on a scouting expedition. His reports were so glowing that in May, 1880, John Mooney, then sixty-eight years old, with his forty-seven-year-old wife, gathered up the family, including six-year-old Nellie, and set out for the Promised Lands. They travelled by boat to Duluth and then by train to St. Boniface, Manitoba, at that time the end of the line.

The decade 1870-80 marked a change from a fur-trade economy to a grain-trade economy for the west. Optimism and confidence were in the very air. Immigrants, mainly from Ontario, were pouring in to take advantage of the incredible growth-potential of the Red River gumbo.

The Mooneys, together with other immigrant families, spent a time in the 'tent city' at The Forks, the junction of the Red and Assiniboine rivers. Here they had the advantages of "city services," such as the butcher's cart which came around twice a week selling steak at 75 cents a pound. They also had a do-it-yourself milk service, courtesy of the two cows which were led through the camp at regular intervals.

Will joined them there, full of his winter's tale. He told them of frost that split the trees with a resounding crack, and of howling wolves, but he also told of winter skies exploding in Northern Lights of unbelievable beauty.

The family spent the summer in a rented house in St. James, just *Immigrant going west*

Red River ox-cart

west of Winnipeg, while John Mooney and sons Will and George went off to build a cabin.

This rented house was next door to a magnificent mansion, "Silver Heights," the home of Donald Smith (Lord Strathcona), one of the men instrumental in building the C.P.R. Many a night the Mooney girls hung out their bedroom windows enjoying the elegant ladies and gentlemen waltzing to violin music next door.

Letitia Mooney could not be happy without a garden and the summer was spent weeding and hoeing in preparation for the onions, beets, carrots and potatoes which were to be "put down" for the winter ahead.

In September 1880, John and Will returned to pick up the family. There was a nearly 300-km trek along the Portage Road and the Yellow Quill Trail ahead of them. They walked, occasionally clambering onto one of the two ox-carts, bulging with the household goods.

These Red River ox-carts were strange, shrieking vehicles peculiar to the region. They were made entirely of wood, as any metal, because of the oil required, tended to collect the prairie dust and slow progress to a final, grinding halt. There were hazards, however, even with this contraption. Dust was not a problem, but grasshoppers were. Nellie wrote of one journey: "We had to scrape the grasshopper pudding off our cart...our wheels were spread over with a batter of grasshopper dough, right up to the hubs and beyond, to the tops of the wheels. We must have helped against the grasshopper plague. Why hadn't Manitobans thought of running a Red River cart tour over the grasshopper locale!"

The Manitoba gumbo was as lethal as quicksand. Travellers on the road could often be seen helping each other free their carts. Sometimes three yokes of oxen were needed to pull one wagon out of a mud-hole. Fifteen kilometres was an average day's travel, and one day they logged only a single kilometre.

At High Bluff, the Mooneys bought a pony and another small cart. They made quite a cavalcade with their two ox-wagons, ponycart, one cow, one dog and six Mooneys.

Bannock was their staple diet. Letitia was expert at making the soft dough of lard, flour, baking powder, salt and milk. She would then press it into a sizzling frying pan in which bacon had been fried, making sure that the pan was covered to keep out the ashes.

After many days on the road, and many meals of bannock, the Mooneys arrived safely at their destination.

Chapter 2
Clearing in the West

When the cavalcade eventually reached the homestead at the junction of Oak Creek, Spring Brook and the Souris River – the beautiful spot which was to be their home for so many years – George was ready for them. Nellie loved the place.

Nellie aged 5

Years later she wrote: "I was one of the children who found the pussy willows, and listened for the first meadow lark, and made little channels with a hoe to let the spring water find its ways to the creek, and ran swift as rabbits when the word went round that the ice was going out of the Souris, and cried if we missed it!"

A few kilometres northeast of them was the town of Millford, where goods were brought by steamboat on the Assiniboine and Souris rivers from Winnipeg. Some years later, frequent and damaging spring floods caused this town to be abandoned. All that remains of Millford today are a few cellar holes and a cairn commemorating the pioneers, with a dedication plaque written by Nellie McClung:

These were the men and women who laid the foundation of this community. They had something that kept them from despair when the crops failed, the cow died, the payment on the binder was due, the children were sick and the nearest doctor was 80 miles away. They trusted in God and went on triumphantly. May we, their descendants, seek to follow their example.

With a lot of hard work and loving care, Will, George and their father had built a house of poplar logs, cornered in the notch-and-saddle style. The rafters and cross pieces of poles raised the roof over gables of logs; then it was thatched with prairie grass. Splendidly, it boasted one window through which the Mooney family could view the outside world.

Years later, Nellie remembered living in that house: "We had home-made bedsteads, made of poplar poles and spread with planks to hold the feather ticks and with plenty of bedding and pillows we slept very comfortably. Sometimes the howling of the prairie wolves drove away sleep and caused me to shudder with fear; there was something so weird and menacing in their shrill prolonged cries, which seemed to rise and fall in a rhythm which brought them nearer and nearer."

In 1882, neighbours gathered to help with the "raising," and a new, larger, two-storey house was built.

The Mooneys were not prosperous, but they were a happy, self-reliant family. Nellie's mother was a wonder at curing colds with turpentine or goose-oil rubs and mustard foot-baths. Her Balm-of-Gilead salve, made from sticky buds of early spring mixed with mutton-tallow and a few drops of carbolic acid, could soothe any wound. In fact Letitia Mooney's home-made remedies were more effective than the alternatives proposed by the peddlers hawking their wares from carts in the town streets – "La-deez and Genulmen..., we have here the Great Swamp Root Bitters which will have you leaping and running as of old... guaranteed to cure floating kidneys, fallen arches, glands in the neck, styes on the eyes, boils, bunions, erosions or eruptions, the pip, the peesy-weesy or the gout!"

Letitia Mooney was equally good at providing the family with appetizing food, using a minimum of ingredients. If the wild saskatoons, raspberries and strawberries were finished and if the hens weren't laying, Letitia produced, without fresh fruit or eggs, delectable pies filled with molasses, butter, bread crumbs, vinegar and cinnamon. She was strict, she was blunt, but she was a Good Samaritan to all and she had a gracious spirit.

Nellie first experienced more prosperous living when a "rich" neighbour gave her a banana and her first taste of chocolate. This was sheer heaven to the little farm girl. Nellie was almost ten when she first started at the new Northfield school and it was there, for the first time, that she felt slightly irked by her family's poverty. Armed with her slate, slate rag and pen wiper, she entered the school wearing dark grey handknitted stockings and a homespun dress. How she longed for "boughten" clothes – they were the real status symbol!

It was a time of hard work, but there was also time for enjoyment. There were many community "bees" when everyone pitched in to help a neighbour raise a house, break fields, or thresh a crop. The Methodist church was built in 1882 entirely by community labour. Community picnics, too, were great occasions for socializing.

John Mooney, an ardent Conservative, held forth loud and long in the frequent political discussions at these community gatherings. Of course, the men did not consider it seemly for women to take part in these discussions – they had their recipes and babies to talk about.

Young Nellie, an opinionated iconoclast from the first, rebelled at this then prevalent male attitude. She was also deeply disturbed by the prevailing female attitude, which held that it was a mistake to educate girls – just making them want to read books instead of patching quilts. There were no races for girls at the picnics, nor were they permitted in the baseball games, played with a yarn ball and barrelstave bat. There was the horrid possibility that their skirts might fly up.

Nellie's despairing cries of why, why, should things be this way forever had no answer.

But there were sound reasons for many women believing that a practical training was the best thing a girl could have: there were so many practical details to attend to in the course of a day.

Even when Nellie was attending school, she still had her part to play in the demanding life of a Manitoba farm. There were always cows to be milked, pigs and hens to be fed, bread to be baked, butter to be churned, potatoes to be peeled, lamp and lantern glasses to be cleaned each day.

Washing clothes was a long and tedious task. Water hauled from the river had to "settle" to eliminate the mud. Melted snow was used in winter. The beef-fat-and-lye homemade soap was scrubbed into the clothes on a washboard. Many times the clean laundry drying on the clothesline or a fence post fell in the mud. Then the whole wearying process had to be repeated.

Ironing was no trifling matter either. The heavy flatirons were heated on the stove, which had to be kept piping hot for so long that bread was usually baked at the same time.

It was no wonder that the only use many women made of the newspaper was to clip recipes from it, or to scallop the edges to decorate their pantry shelves.

It was in these early years too that Nellie became disenchanted with the way people abused their power. She could never believe that might made right. Machinery was being introduced on the farms, and several of the settlers had optimistically bought binders, all of which turned out to be faulty. In answer to their many reasonable letters to the big implement company, the settlers got

Nellie in her teens

absolutely no satisfaction. In fact, the final letter from the business moguls said, among other rude comments, "No machine can do good work in the hands of bungling operators, and unfortunately we cannot supply brains, our business is machinery."

A school friend remembers Nellie as a willful, stubborn young lady, brooking no interference. He says: "I went to the one outhouse in the schoolyard, flung open the door and got the surprise of my life. A quick, hard, well-placed kick to my stomach knocked me back reeling. I was reeling too from the language Miss Nellie Mooney used in telling me to leave."

No doubt she was practising her language skills in preparation for a literary career.

A strangely lugubrious beginning to that career was made when she was twelve:

> Four dead dogs, they died alone
> Nobody saw them or heard them groan,
> There they died by the drifts of snow
> While the wind rocked their tails to and fro.

Although she was usually a merry youngster, there were days when Nellie was despondent. Her particular chore was to keep the cattle out of the unfenced fields of growing grain. It was a pleasant enough chore in summer, but when school started in August, and she watched others trundling off to their learning while she was tending the cattle, the "darkness of the pit" was in her soul. Her schooling was a chancy thing at best. But eventually the fields were fenced and she was able to attend more regularly.

In spite of a world-wide economic depression, declining farm prices and industrial stagnation, in the Manitoba countryside there was just no such thing as unemployment. There were never enough hands to do the work. One woman who had an unwelcome summer house-guest said: "I would not have put up with her sauce only I knew I needed her in threshing-time."

Immigrants were still being encouraged to settle in the west. Farmers registered at the railway office, agreeing to pay hired hands $5 a month and teach them farming into the bargain. Many were the British younger sons who flocked west, to the land of milk and honey, without even a rudimentary knowledge of how to persuade the cow to release her milk, or the bees their honey. They did, however, introduce a whole new dimension of culture to the Manitoba countryside. Some had "book-learning" and brought their books with them; others were highly-accomplished musicians or artists, and they enlarged the horizons of the practical farming families.

Life, of necessity, was practical. One young bachelor wrote home: "I hope to marry – some lady well versed in scrubbing, washing, baking, dairying, getting up at 3:30 in summer, 5:50 in winter; strong nerves, strong constitution, obedient, and with money."

As time went on, the Mooneys became more prosperous – a carpet in the livingroom, chintz curtains on the windows and real blinds, a silk eiderdown on the master bed. But economies still had to be practised, with eggs fetching only ten cents a dozen and butter eighteen a pound.

In July, 1889, Nellie passed exams in Brandon which made her eligible to train as a teacher at the Normal School in Winnipeg. But all seemed lost when frost came early to the prairies and the Mooneys' crop was wiped out. Her sister Hannah, however, now teaching at Indian Head west of Brandon, and her other sister, Lizzie, were determined that young Nell would make it to the city and came forward with offers to finance her.

And so, Nellie Mooney, not yet sixteen, set off at 5 o'clock one morning for the metropolis of Winnipeg – a full day's journey. The cash for a month's board and for schoolbooks was prudently sewn into her undergarments. She felt very grown-up and splendid in her green dress "with brass buttons and bound with military braid." Her buttoned boots were of fine goatskin. Her stockings were black cashmere. As a proper young lady she wore two petticoats – a crocheted one and a white one over it. She also had a homemade "cloud" to wear in the cold weather but it was the cause of some anguish: "When I found that most of the girls at the Normal had fur collars on their coats I grew very much ashamed of my 'cloud' and did not wear it until both ears had been frozen."

Letitia Mooney was always warning Nellie that her pride would come before a fall.

Chapter 3
Beginnings

Sir Clifford Sifton

Winnipeg in the 1890s

Winnipeg was a city full of excitement in those days, especially for a young girl leaving home for the first time to begin her own career. Winnipeg, and indeed the whole of western Canada, was expanding at a fantastic rate. The C.P.R. had been completed in 1885, but it was not until Clifford Sifton entered the scene that the west really began to grow.

In the closing decade of the nineteenth century, western Canada became the new mecca for the old world. Clifford Sifton of Winnipeg, Prime Minister Laurier's Minister of the Interior from 1896 to 1905, scattered throughout Europe seductive pamphlets in twenty languages praising the grain-growing excellence of Red River gumbo. Immigrants poured into Manitoba and further west. Sifton had neglected to mention the chill winter winds, the killing frosts and flailing hail on the prairies.

Winnipeg was booming. By the early 1900s, twelve railway lines converged there. The Grain Exchange had been founded in 1887 to service the prairie wheatland. People, goods and services all funneled through the city. Winnipegers were full of confidence and boundless optimism.

When the fifteen-year-old Nellie Mooney arrived there in 1889, wide-eyed from the farm, Winnipeg, Gateway to the West, was already a metropolis.

Exhilaration was in the sharp winter air. The uneven clip-clop of horses' feet pulling street-cars and cutters made an interesting obbligato to the clang of the street-cars, the jingle of the silver bells on the cutters, and the rowdy, good-natured shouts of the people on the wide, crowded streets. It was a world of sound and colour. Red flannel edges on the sleighs' buffalo robes, green, gold and red bottles in drugstore windows illuminated by hanging coal-oil lanterns, all blended into a dizzying kaleidoscope.

Her year at the Normal School was an exciting one for Nellie – one in which the whole world of books opened out before her. Occasionally during her year of teacher-training, Nellie earned three dollars a day as a teaching substitute, and at the end of the year, she was qualified as a public school teacher. The principal's parting words to the graduating class were, "Demand decent salaries and wear clean linen."

Nellie's first school was at Somerset, where she was to teach all eight grades. Somerset was a whistle-stop 28 kilometres from Manitou, which was about fifty kilometres south-west of Winnipeg. The home of the school trustee with whom she was to board was only five kilometres from Manitou.

When the trustee met her at the station, he was quick to tell her that the crop had been flattened to the ground by hail and she would not be getting any pay after all. She would get her board and room and she'd better "eat hearty," because that way she'd be getting paid more.

Nellie had always been a religious girl, and during her time in Somerset, she went to church with the trustee and his family in Manitou. Nellie was utterly captivated by the new minister's wife who taught the Young Ladies' Bible Class: "She is the only woman I have ever seen whom I should like to have for a mother-in-law." That woman's name was McClung.

Later, when she heard that there was an eighteen-year-old

Looking for land

McClung, Wes, who had just completed a study term in the east, and was now working in the Manitou drugstore, Nellie dressed herself in her best, put her last three dollars in her pocket, and made a foray into town to have a look. She would buy a fountain pen from Wes. She liked what she saw: "a tall, slim young fellow with clear blue eyes and clear skin." Deferring to him, she spent some considerable time in choosing just the right pen. Those last three dollars were spent on what was probably the most significant purchase of her life.

Nellie McClung never did believe that it was fair that a woman should sit around waiting for a man to notice her. Why couldn't a woman make the first move? She was equally unconventional as a teacher. At school – heedless of her skirts – she played football with her pupils as energetically as she pursued every activity. Her charges also claimed she had "the magic:" she would forecast futures by feeling the bumps on their heads. No doubt this accomplishment helped to pass the time while the students sat still as Nellie barbered them. She brought the "magic" to the theatre too and produced a Christmas concert which was a smashing success.

That Christmas of 1889 she received a present of the complete works of Charles Dickens. Dickens was to become one of the most

profound influences in her life: "As I read," she later recalled, "... a light shone around me. I knew... what a writer can be... an interpreter, a revealer of secrets, a heavenly surgeon, a sculptor who can bring an angel out of a stone... I wanted to do for the people around me what Dickens had done for his people."

Methodist Church, Manitou

Nellie had already begun to write regularly herself: one giant scribbler after another was filled with her impressions of events, her ideas, and her innermost thoughts. The habit, begun so early, never left her. Reading Dickens reinforced her determination to use these writings some day, easily confident that the whole world was waiting for her story.

Her confidence proved to be well-founded. Nellie did become a writer of some fame, publishing a total of sixteen books and numerous articles. She never forgot the habit she acquired during her early life: all her books were written in longhand, usually in pencil.

E. Cora Hind

Nellie McClung's home in Manitou

When her teaching salary reached forty dollars a month Nellie was able to buy books – her greatest treat. She knew it was impossible to be a writer unless she was first a reader.

Nellie was encouraged in her writing by the example of E. Cora Hind, the first public stenographer west of the Great Lakes. It was a red-letter day for Nellie when Cora Hind came to town. Nellie made a point of being at the Manitou station to meet her. She was overcome with admiration for the neat, well-dressed young woman who actually sold articles to the Winnipeg Free Press.

A friendship was established between the two women which lasted through the years, the kind of friendship which is picked up easily no matter how much time elapses. Later, Cora Hind reviewed Nellie's books for the newspaper and, whether favourable or unfavourable, the review never affected their great friendship.

In the fall of 1892, Nellie got a teaching job at the Manitou School – a step up the ladder, since Manitou was highly regarded as a centre of learning, boasting as it did one of the three provincial Normal Schools. She boarded at the parsonage with the McClungs, and she didn't mind that at all!

Beginnings

Chapter 4
Liquor and Love

Life was going well for Nellie Mooney. At nineteen, she had already completed two successful years of teaching, and had made a start at her writing. Now, in Manitou in 1892, she was furthering her career – and her social life.

It was a happy time – hayrides, tally-hos, dances, skating parties for the young people. There were no telephones, radios, movies, daily papers or lending libraries, but there was plenty of fun.

It was also a time in which Nellie's desire for social change, and for equal rights for women, was finding a positive direction, largely because of Mrs. McClung's influence. Mrs. McClung was a remarkable woman, years ahead of her time in her thinking. It was she who led Nellie to the Women's Christian Temperance Union, as an outlet for her temperance activities.

Temperance, originally meaning "moderation," by now had the accepted meaning of "total abstinence" – that is, the giving up of all alcoholic drinks.

In those days in rural Manitoba, ladies simply did not drink, and men were apparently divided into those who were teetotalers (that is, who never took a drink) and those who were drunkards. Nellie's mother, Letitia Mooney, had always held that liquor was the devil's device for confounding mankind. Nellie herself had vivid memories of community picnics ending in utter shambles because of drunken men.

The Women's Christian Temperance Union had been founded in Cleveland, Ohio, in 1874. Socially conscious women all across North America were becoming despairingly aware of the unhappiness caused by drunkenness. Liquor all too often led to violence, and to economic hardship for a man's family; it was innocent women and children who suffered the most from drink. Writing in 1915, Nellie reported that in one year alone in the United States, 3,000 women had been murdered by their drunken husbands. She unearthed statistics showing that the majority of children born to heavy drinkers were abnormal in some way. The problems caused by liquor were truly of gigantic proportions; Nellie always hoped that when women got the vote, prohibition would be introduced.

Winnipeg Collegiate Institute

In 1877, women in Manitoba, desperate at the thousands of dollars gurgling down their men's gullets each year, founded the Ladies Temperance Union Society, which became a branch of the WCTU. Nellie became an enthusiastic member in Manitou, and continued her fervour throughout her life.

The WCTU not only fought for temperance, but also operated as a place where women could air their views. In the WCTU Reading and Amusement Room in Manitou, where coffee was available at two cups for fifteen cents, many debates were thrashed out. Should Canada become part of the United States? Is it possible to live without sin? No subject was too formidable for these women to tackle.

Nellie spent the winter of 1893 at the Collegiate Institute in Winnipeg, upgrading for her First-Class Teacher's certificate. When she was posted the next year to teach at Treherne, a village of six hundred, she immediately became a member of the WCTU Mission Board there. Oddly enough, none other than Mr. McClung had the church at Treherne at this time. Wes was still in Manitou, about fifty kilometres away, but visited his family frequently – not to mention the village schoolteacher.

Nellie's work on the Mission Board gave her the opportunity to teach temperance to the young. On one occasion, she led a group of children – her little "Band of Hope," all dressed in their Sunday best – in a march. They passed the hotel, where Nellie directed their gaze toward the men enjoying their beer on the verandah. Encouraged by Nellie, the children sang their piping best:

Down with whisky all
Vote it down, vote it down.
Death to old King Alcohol
Vote it down, vote it down.

Single-minded deter-
mination marked all of
Nellie's activities: it was
evident in her campaign
against alcohol, and she
applied it with equal relish
to her relationship with
Wes McClung. She had set
her cap for him in Manitou.
She had found a man who
agreed with her ideas on
women's rights, who appre-
ciated her ability to argue
intelligently, her quick wit,
her lively pretty face. And
what's more, they had fallen
in love. They walked for
hours together discussing
theology, philosophy and
literature. While Wes was
studying for his pharmacy
degree in Toronto and
Nellie was at the Collegiate
in Winnipeg, they
exchanged weekly letters.

Nellie and Wes McClung

During the winter of 1895-96 Nellie taught at her own old
school, Northfield. In January, Wes came to visit her family and get
to know the Mooney neighbours. He fitted in like the final piece of
a jigsaw puzzle. One friend's approving comment was, "That man
can do a lot of washing in a very few suds."

On the stormy morning of August 25th, 1896, while the wind
was raging, Nellie and Wes were married. They boarded the train to
the rattle of hailing rain. A few kilometres along the track, however,
the rain stopped abruptly and the wind dropped. The Manitoba sun
burst forth in all its glory – clearly a good omen.

Chapter 5
Babies and Books

The young couple started their new life together in a four-room apartment over the Manitou drugstore, which Wes now owned.

Nellie's tremendous curiosity and genuine interest in people made her the listening post for the people of Manitou. Many of the tales they told of their own experiences sparked short stories in later years. Nellie was consciously trying to learn the writer's craft: she was reading voraciously, analyzing as she went, in order to ferret out the formula for a good story.

When she was pregnant with her first child, Nellie once again pondered on the burdens borne by women: "Why has something not been done to relieve this infernal nausea? If it were a man's disease it would have been made the subject of scientific research and relieved long ago." When little Jack was born on June 16th, 1897, however, Nellie said that "the most exquisite moment I have ever known" was when the baby was placed at her side. Three more children were born in Manitou – Florence in 1899, Paul in 1901, and Horace in 1906.

The people of Manitou enjoyed a good show. All nine hundred of them would turn out in full force to see any travelling artists or road shows, and local talent was always assured of a full house. They loved a good speaker.

Nellie McClung was the main speaker at a WCTU provincial convention in Manitou in 1907. Realizing that her topic – "prohibition" – had a harsh sound for a rallying cry and might not "fire the heather," she dressed in her best and gave of her best.

For the first time she experienced the heady feeling that the power of eloquence can give, when faces brighten, eyes glisten and the atmosphere crackles at one's words. She was bitten with the bug forever. She could chuckle at herself though. In a novel she wrote: "Wherever two or three gather together, Pearl Watson [her autobiographical character] will rise and make a few remarks unless someone forcibly restrains her."

The WCTU was a tremendous force in rural Manitoba. Among its many other activities, it gave temperance talks in the schools.

At one of these talks, Nellie, using the show-and-tell method, placed two large glasses on the desk. Into one she poured water, into the other, strong drink. She dropped a limp worm into the water – it immediately perked up and swam strongly. Into the other glass she dropped a second worm which promptly sank to the bottom, victim of the lethal dose. "And what does this teach us, class?" said school-marm Nellie. In the twinkling of an eye, a bright young lad called out, "If you drink whisky, you'll never get worms!"

As time went on, it was recognized in rural Manitoba that when-ever Nellie was to speak, it was prudent to bring one's own chair. An old-timer recalls: "Nellie McClung lit up like a candle when she

Nellie in 1908

spoke." In later years, when the name "Windy Nell" was in lights over Massey Hall in Toronto, it was a guarantee that, not only would it be Standing Room Only, but thousands would be turned away. The fact that there were no amplifiers in those days did not keep anyone, even at the back of the hall, from hearing her ringing voice, or from feeling the force of her personal magnetism.

Suffragettes and temperance workers elsewhere sometimes resorted to violence to get their message across. There was the case of Carrie Nation who, in 1900, wrecked Dobson's Saloon in Kansas, leaving the place awash in beer and broken glasses. This was never Nellie's way: she preferred witty and gently cutting remarks. Heckled at a temperance meeting once by a character who said: "Don't you wish you were a man right now, Nellie?" she flashed back, "Don't you wish you were?"

These were crowded years for Nellie – she was gaining a reputation as a public speaker, she was raising three small children, and she was pursuing her writing career – encouraged once again by Mrs. McClung senior. In 1902, Nellie's mother-in-law, feeling that "life conspires to keep a woman tangled in trifles," offered to help with the children while Nellie wrote. It was Mrs. McClung who first introduced Nellie to the publishing world by virtually insisting that she enter a short story contest run by *Collier's*, a popular American magazine. Months later, the story came winging back to her with a note of rejection. In the meantime, however, her self-confidence had been bolstered by the appearance of several of her articles and stories in the Methodist Sunday School publications.

She sent the story off again. It surfaced from an editor's "slush pile" of unsolicited manuscripts in 1905, and was returned to her with the suggestion that it be enlarged into a novel. *Sowing Seeds in Danny* was published in 1908, became the bestseller of the year in Canada, went into seventeen editions, eventually sold over 100,000 copies and earned almost $25,000 for the author. This was a most unusual accomplishment in a society so recently removed from a pre-occupation with survival, rather than with the arts.

Strictly speaking, Nellie's works could not be described as great art. They had a closer relationship to soap-opera. Nurtured on Dickens and on the melodramatic "Gothic" tales which were serialized in the *Family Herald* newspaper, Nellie was an incurable romantic. Pearl Watson, the heroine of *Sowing Seeds in Danny* and of its sequel, *The Second Chance* (1910), was a thinly-disguised Nellie McClung. Her strength was as the strength of ten, because her heart was pure.

Once again Mrs. McClung got to work on Nellie's behalf and made arrangements for her to give readings in Winnipeg from

Sowing Seeds in Danny as a moneyraiser for the WCTU. In pre-radio and pre-television times, readings were popular social happenings.

For her first reading, Nellie got a new soft blue dress. She had a hair-do, a manicure and a facial. She even went so far as to let the operator use some rouge on her creamy-white cheeks, a radical departure from her usual practice of scrubbing a rose-leaf from an old hat on them.

Not only were the readings popular in Winnipeg, there was a great demand throughout rural Manitoba too. But not quite a universal demand. Nellie loved to tell about the youngster in one town who rushed out of the drugstore when Nellie entered. Chided later by his mother, he said, "That awful speaker woman was in the store and she isn't going to get a chance to sow any seeds in me!"

Fan-mail began to come in from all her audiences. One male admirer wrote her:

Hail Prairie Rose
Sweetest flower that blows
Winsome, winning – never shinning
Handsome, chic – verbose!

Nellie remarked with a twinkle that the last word had quite obviously been inserted merely "to complete the rhyme."

Not everything she received was as flattering. Some of her mail that was addressed to the WCTU interpreted the abbreviation as Women Continually Torment Us. There are always people who have no love for an alarm clock.

Nellie was not a scold. She was an alarm clock, but she was also a warm, compassionate woman, always ready to help others with their problems.

Not far out of Manitou lived a solitary bachelor who bred dogs. Every time a buggy went past, the animals raised a deafening uproar. When this became too much for him, or the loneliness of his life preyed on his mind, he would get helplessly drunk. Everyone in town knew that Nellie would care for him when this happened. He was eternally grateful for her care and concern. Some years later, Nellie heard from a minister that the old bachelor felt that it was because of her that he had finally been able to lick the drinking habit. It had now been years since the man had touched liquor, and the minister was writing to let Nellie know that her help and prayers had not been in vain.

The years in Manitou were happy, successful ones for the McClungs. Nellie, not yet forty years old, was fast becoming a celebrity – as a writer (two of her books had been published), reader, public speaker, temperance worker, and advocate of women's rights. She had four children of her own, and many of the children of the town flocked to Nellie's door – to get elocution lessons, be rehearsed for Christmas concerts, or simply to have their "bumps read." She still had the "magic."

Then, in 1911, Wes received an attractive offer from a life insurance company. He sold the drugstore, and the family moved to Winnipeg.

Chapter 6
In Times Like These

I t was the best of times. In the years before the outbreak of
World War I, Winnipeg was the transportation and manufactur-
ing hub of the Canadian west. New industries were burgeoning,
old ones were experiencing explosive growth. Among these, in spite
of the doughty efforts of the WCTU, was the brewing industry.
The first primitive brewery had opened in the Winnipeg area in
1860. By 1904, sales had passed the five million litre mark, and by
1914, the level of 25 million litres – what some might consider a
profit without honour.

It was also the worst of times. An eligible voter in Canada was

*Manitoba Equal Suffrage Club
about 1900*

defined as "a male person, including an Indian and excluding a person of Mongolian or Chinese race... No woman, idiot, lunatic or criminal shall vote."

Ladies were educated to sew, bake, play the organ, and to make quilts and seed-wreaths. Equal pay for equal work was unheard-of for women in the work force. It was worse than that: a woman's salary was legally the property of her husband. The law gave him the control of their children and the right to beat his wife at his whim. An unmarried mother had absolute control of her children, but the rights of a married mother during the life of the father while she was living with him were not recognized by law. Only the father's consent was necessary for the marriage of a minor child. The Married Women's Protection Act of 1902 protected women against drunkenness, neglect, desertion and cruelty, but a married woman who had committed an act of adultery could not obtain an order of protection under this Act. No protection order, however, could be given to the wife permitting her to live apart from her husband on the grounds of the husband's adultery. Women were the inarticulate sex. Books about women were written by men. They were idealized in novels, and treated with contempt in law. Women, of course, had no voice in the making of such laws. It was a state of affairs that most of the men in power had no desire to change, and they were quick to find justification for the status quo.

CWPC Annual Meeting, 1906

In Times Like These

In 1893, commenting on a suffrage resolution introduced in the Ontario Legislature, one minister clinched its rejection by quoting - the Bible: "Thy desire shall be to thy husband and he shall rule over thee."

Manitoba was faced with the same kind of opposition. In 1894, the WCTU, with a petition of two thousand names, had managed to get a women's suffrage bill introduced into the Manitoba Legislature. But when it was called for second reading, its promoter, a faint-hearted man ironically named Mr. Ironside, simply mumbled, "Not printed." The bill was still-born.

CWPC clubroom about 1912

Winnipeg society, like that everywhere, was male-dominated. But in 1911, Nellie McClung burst onto the scene. Although her fifth child, Mark, had just been born, she was "not content with punching holes in linen and sewing them up again" or "making butterfly medallions for my camisoles." She joined the Canadian Women's Press Club, which was deeply concerned with women's rights. This organization, founded in Winnipeg, was the first national press women's body in the world. Through membership in the club, Nellie became one of a gaggle of "liberated" women, including her friend, E. Cora Hind. Cora was now agricultural editor of the *Free Press*, and her crop predictions were eagerly awaited all over the world. The group also included Kennethe Haig and Lillian Beynon Thomas, both editorial writers. Nellie and her cohorts felt that with a strong women's club movement, they would get women outside the home, and, with the vote, into the political arena where the female moral superiority would be a valuable part of the decision-making process.

At their weekly meetings, they passionately discussed women's suffrage and women's rights generally. There was much to discuss: women suffered from discrimination everywhere. Females, for instance, could be insured "against death only," whereas men could

Sir Rodmond Roblin

be insured against illness, disfigurement or death. Injustices towards females were the order of the day. There was the case of the farmer, for example, who bequeathed his three farms to his three sons. To his dear daughter Martha he left one hundred dollars and a cow named Bella – "How would you like to be left at forty years of age, with no training and very little education, facing the world with one hundred dollars and one cow, even if she were named 'Bella?'" Nellie asked. The man's widow was designated to receive her "keep" with her youngest son, but nothing else. The assumption was that a woman of sixty-five does not require any spending money. There was no legal recourse for either of these women.

A visit from Emmeline Pankhurst and Barbara Wiley, militant British suffragettes, fired the Women's Press Club with fresh enthusiasm.

Some definite steps had to be taken to improve women's lot, and working women were to be the first target. The group decided to work with the Local Council of Women to help women factory workers.

The Local Council was a branch of the National Council of Women founded in 1893 by Lady Aberdeen, wife of the Governor-General, for the purpose of "applying the Golden Rule to society, custom and the law." Nellie and Mrs. Claude Nash were deputized by the Local Council to approach the Conservative Premier of Manitoba, Sir Rodmond Roblin, to make him aware of the rotten working conditions of female factory workers, and to press for the appointment of a woman factory inspector. They persuaded him to take them to the "scene of the crime" in his car – a splendid vehicle, with a real carnation in its wall-hung, cut-glass vase.

On the way, snug in his beaver coat, with his plump hands folded over his gold-headed cane, he lectured them on their folly in mixing in this nasty hurly-burly world. On being told the factory hands worked from 8:30 a.m. to 6 p.m., six days a week with no sick leave, he replied, "No doubt they get used to it, they want the pin money and if they're sick they can always quit."

The women escorted him down the dark slippery stairs to an airless, unheated basement, the floor of which was covered with apple peelings and discarded clothing. They made him take a good look round. What really appalled him was the single toilet – no sex discrimination here. It was apparent to the least sensitive nostril that something had gone awry with the plumbing. Gasping, "For God's sake, let me out of here, I'm choking! I never knew such hell-holes existed," Sir Rodmond stumbled up the stairs.

Would he appoint a trained woman social worker as a factory inspector, Nellie asked. An unequivocal "No!" was the reply. He had "too much respect for women to give them that kind of a job." The visit that they had planned as a prelude to legislative action simply reinforced his belief that "nice" ladies wouldn't involve themselves in such utterly disgusting matters.

Unfortunately, he was partially correct in this assumption: the Local Council itself had many establishment members who refused to rock the boat for fear of censure from their husbands. It became necessary to form a new group which was prepared to press for legislative action. Some of the fearless members, including Nellie, E. Cora Hind, Francis Beynon, Lillian Beynon Thomas, Kennethe Haig and Dr. Mary Crawford, formed the Political Equality League in 1912. The League was dedicated to female suffrage. They were joined in their efforts toward this end by the WCTU, the Icelandic Women's Suffrage Association, the Grain Growers' Association and the Women's Labour League.

The stout-hearted suffragettes in Canada were supported by some males who were undaunted by the chilling prospect of women actually voting. L. Case Russell wrote ironically in the Toronto *Globe*, September 28th, 1912:

> *You may be our close companion*
> > *Share our troubles, ease our pain,*
> *You may bear the servant's burden*
> > *(But without a servant's gain)*
> *You may scrub and work and iron*
> > *Sew buttons on our coat*
> *But as men we must protect you—*
> > *You are far too frail to vote.*
> *You may toil behind our counters*
> > *In our factories you may slave*
> *You are welcome in the sweatshops*
> > *From the cradle to the grave.*
> *If you err, altho' a woman*
> > *You may dangle by the throat*
> *But our chivalry is outraged*
> > *If you soil your hands to vote.*

Emmeline Parkhurst (centre) with Nellie McClung (left) and Emily Murphy (right)

Nellie always did regard "chivalry" as "a poor substitute for justice... something like the icing on cake, sweet but not nourishing."

Chapter 7
Suffragists

The suffrage movement was gaining impetus in Manitoba, but prejudice was still strong – and there was still Sir Rodmond to content with. Nellie had one memorable interview with the Premier in which she had to suffer his amused tolerance as he aired his views: "I don't want a hyena in petticoats talking politics at me. I want a nice gentle creature to bring me my slippers."

It was too much for Nellie McClung. She stomped out of his office snapping, "You'll hear from me again and you may not like it!"

"Is this a threat?" asked the Premier.

"No," replied Calamity Nell, "it's a prophecy."

On January 27th, 1914, a delegation led by Nellie presented its case for female suffrage to the Manitoba Legislature. The delegation represented the Political Equality League, the Icelandic Women's Suffrage Association, the Grain Growers' Association, the Women's Christian Temperance Union, the Trades and Labour Council, the Canadian Women's Press Club and the Young Women's Christian Association. The Premier was as stubborn as ever. Nellie marked, learned and inwardly digested every word, every gesture, as Sir Rodmond fulminated at his foamy best:

> "Let it be known that it is the opinion of the Roblin government that woman suffrage is illogical and absurd as far as Manitoba is concerned. Placing women on a political equality with men would cause domestic strife. Sex antagonism would be aroused. It is an easy flame to fan. I believe that woman suffrage would be a retrograde movement, that it will break up the home, that it will throw the children into the arms of servant girls... The majority of women are emotional and very often guided by mis-directed enthusiasm, and if possessed of the franchise would be a menace rather than an aid. It is not right nor is it wise to intro-duce into our form of government constitutional feminine tem-perament."

Our Nell, as a child, had left her father helpless with laughter in the Mooneys' own private theatre – the barn – as she burlesqued her mother's rather prissy Presbyterian aunts. Our Nell was the youngster always chosen to be Chief Poundmaker when the children acted out the 1885 Rebellion. She revelled in making speeches about waving grass, running streams, waning moons and setting suns. Our Nell was now about to do her biggest star turn.

The night after Roblin had made his speech, it echoed in the Walker Theatre before a full house. There, under the auspices of the Political Equality League, the women staged a Mock Parliament – a vice-versa situation in which the entire membership of the Legislature was female. Even the pages running busily about were little girls, including, naturally, the fourteen-year-old Florence McClung.

Petitions were presented, motions were moved, questions were asked, and bills were read. There was a bill to confer dower rights (the right to property after the death of a spouse) on married men. There was a measure to give fathers equal guardianship rights with mothers. The women had a great time hamming it up.

Walker Theatre

The climax of the session was the arrival of a delegation of men petitioning for suffrage, plaintively crying, "We have the brains – why not let us vote?"

The "Premier," Nellie McClung, teetering back and forth in a perfect parody of Roblin's gestures, brought down the house with her lengthy reply to the male upstarts:

"The trouble is that if men start to vote, they will vote too much. Politics unsettles men, and unsettled men means unsettled bills, broken furniture, broken vows and – divorce... It has been charged that politics is corrupt. I do not know how this report got out but I do most emphatically deny it. I have been in politics for a long time and I never knew of any division of public money among the members of the House, and you may be sure, if anything of the kind had been going on, I should have been in on it...

"If men were to get into the habit of voting – who knows what might happen – it's hard enough to keep them home now. History is full of unhappy examples of men in public life – Nero – Herod – King John...

"Some men become so hypnotized by politics that they return from the grave to vote..." *(It had been alleged that voters' lists in the Premier's riding included some names from tombstones.)*

And so it went. The whole affair was a smashing success – the theatre was packed to capacity – the press notices were great:
"Sir Rodmond's Weak Position Assailed by Winnipeg Women and his Old-fashioned Theories Exploded..."
"Woman Suffragists Gambol at Walker Theatre..."
"Women Score in Drama and Debate..."
"Choicest Piece of Satire that has Ever Been Heard Locally."

There was an election shortly after, and the Political Equality League threw itself into the campaign on the Liberal side. The Liberal leader, Norris, had given his support to female suffrage. The Conservatives burned Nellie in effigy. But the women of the League were consumed "not by rage, but by passion." They would do battle against ignorance, isolation, loneliness and ugliness.

Large crowds assembled whenever Nellie was scheduled to speak, and the press always gave her good coverage. Newspapers in June and July of 1914 often included reports such as: "*Crowds Flock to Hear Woman. Mrs. McClung is the magnet that draws thousands to the Walker Theatre. She came, she saw, she conquered thousands...*" But in spite of Nellie's incredible charisma, and all the League's prodigious efforts, in that election of July 10th, 1914, the Conservatives won by a whisker, and again formed the government.

A post-election editorial in *The Grain Growers' Guide* commented: "It is acknowledged throughout Manitoba that the most powerful speeches of the recent political campaign were made by a woman, Mrs. Nellie McClung. Thousands of ignorant and degraded men had votes and some of them, it is reported, voted several times. But there was no ballot for Mrs. McClung."

What did this kind of campaigning do to Nellie's home life? Suffragettes were often criticized for neglecting their families in favour of their other activities. But Nellie was supported in all her toil and travail outside the home by Wes and their five children – Jack, 17, Florence, 15, Paul, 13, Horace, 8, and Mark, 3. They could afford to have household help – often immigrant girls (to whom Nellie taught English on the side). Not only was Wes financially secure, but Nellie's books, which could be counted on to be best-sellers, brought in a considerable income. Her third book, a collection of short stories called *The Black Creek Stopping House*, had been published in 1912.

The McClungs' home life was so secure that they could afford to

Nellie with Mark

mock any accusations to the contrary. When Mark was three, Wes taught him to say, "My name is Mark McClung. I am the son of a suffragette and have never known a mother's love." This lisping admission made a tremendous hit at the tea-parties and gatherings of writers, suffragettes and other friends, which were a feature of the McClung household.

Horace once smuggled an untidy, muddy young Mark down a back lane and back into the house to prevent some nosy reporter from making capital of a "neglected" child.

Florence (McClung) Atkinson says any talk of neglect was "utter nonsense – we had a very happy home life." Nellie with her "gift of the gab" brought all her travels home to her family in "living colour." There were always bedtime stories for the children, frequently readings from Dickens. As Francis M. Beynon pointed out in *The Grain Growers' Guide*, a woman did not have to be a suffragette to "neglect" her home:

No, it isn't home-neglecting
If you spend your time selecting
Seven blouses and a jacket and a hat
Or to give your day to paying
Needless visits, or to playing
Auction bridge. What critic could object to that?
But to spend the precious hours
At a lecture! Oh my powers!
The home is all a woman needs to learn.
And an hour or a quarter
Spent in voting! Why my daughter,
The home would not be there on your return.

Nellie never went on stage to speak without first checking out the home-front, then reassuring her audience that all was well. Asked once if she did not believe a mother's place was in the home, Nellie shot back, "Yes, I do and so is father's – but not twenty-four hours a day for either of them. Woman's duty lies not only in rearing children but also in the world into which those children must some day enter."

In spite of setbacks and accusations, Nellie maintained what she called her "queer streak of cheerful imbecility" and kept fighting fearlessly for what she believed to be right.

Chapter 8
World War and Women's War

The Canadian National Exhibition billed 1914 as "Peace Year," but 1914 turned out to be just the reverse.

The ugliness of war was everywhere: it stamped the men in the trenches, and it spilled over onto Canadian city streets, where self-righteous young women handed white feathers – symbols of cowardice – to any young men not observably disabled. The ugliness of war even filtered down to small children, who shouted "Dirty Hun!" at Canadians with German names.

Women at work in British Munitions Co. Ltd., Verdun, Quebec

Life on the home-front changed dramatically. Factories of all kinds stepped up production. Goods which had formerly come from England now had to be manufactured in Canada. Men were leaving their homes to enlist. By August 18th, 1914, Military District No. 10 in Manitoba had recruited over 5,500 officers and men for the Canadian Expeditionary Force. War took the able-bodied, leaving the unfit and the women to take care of production at home. Women began entering the work force in greater numbers than ever before. "Rosie the Riveter" learned to enjoy a pay cheque, and

T.C. Norris

was disinclined to return to being "just a housewife" after the war.

The pressure on farmers and farmers' wives to feed the Allies was tremendous. Two-dollar wheat became the order of the day. Nellie commented that "the high colour of prosperity on the cheek of agriculture is not the glow of health but the flush of fever."

1914 was also a year of change for the McClung family. In December, the Manufacturers Life Insurance Company transferred Wes to Edmonton as manager for northern Alberta. Although she was sad to leave Winnipeg, Nellie was always ready for new doors to open and was soon in the thick of things in her new home. Her brother, Will, who lived in Edmonton with his family, took her to task: "The world isn't ready to accept advice from women... can't you pipe down?... I get tired telling people that you and Wes get on well, and you have no personal reasons for raising such a dust about the liquor traffic and the burdens of women..."

Nellie countered that it was precisely because of her happy marriage that she had a responsibility to work for others: "I never could believe that minding one's own business was much of a virtue, but it's a fine excuse for doing nothing." The "do-nothing" label could never be pinned on Nellie McClung.

Nothing dampened her enthusiasm, and no amount of personal abuse could subdue her. Heckled at one meeting about being in the pay of the Liberals, Nellie retorted: "The Liberal Party doesn't need to pay me when a generous-minded open-faced Conservative like yourself pays fifty cents to hear me."

In her financial dealings, in fact, she was above reproach. Between 1913 and 1921 she addressed more than four hundred public meetings and received actual fees in only three cases. Those fees she donated to good causes.

Politics was generally conceded to be a dirty game. In the Manitoba federal by-elections prior to the 1914 provincial election, vicious charges and countercharges of bribery and false-voting had been savagely flung about. And there was provincial scandal as well. Construction had started on the new Legislative Building in 1913. By the next year, tongues were wagging about faulty construction and slack supervision. In spite of this, the Conservatives squeaked through to form the government. Early in 1915, however, the Liberals were demanding an independent inquiry into the Legislative Building project. The Premier refused to have an investigation, but the Lieutenant-Governor appointed a Royal Commission.

By May the Commission had revealed enough slime under the Conservative rock to induce Sir Rodmond to resign. On May 13th, 1915, T.C. Norris and the Liberals formed the government. A second Royal Commission found that not only had "large sums" been paid to the Provincial Conservative Association, but that the contractor for the elegant Greco-Roman structure on Broadway had been over-paid by almost $900,000, with which little nest-egg he had decamped to the United States.

Innumerable court cases implicated many of Sir Rodmond's colleagues, and not until June, 1917, was the personal integrity of Sir Rodmond established by the courts.

In the provincial election of August, 1915, the Norris government, supported by Nellie McClung and the Political Equality League,

Sir Robert L. Borden

now headed by Dr. Mary Crawford, was confirmed by a landslide vote. (Manitoba had had its last Conservative government until Duff Roblin, the grandson of Sir Rodmond, was elected premier in 1958.)

The fight for women's suffrage continued at the provincial and federal levels. When the Prime Minister, Sir Robert Borden, visited Winnipeg, Nellie, brash as ever, confronted him with these words: "We feel that we should have the franchise given to us without any further agitation, for we are too busy to fight for it, and we will greatly begrudge the time if we have to do so."

The arguments against female suffrage were weak, and Nellie was quick to ridicule them. One of her favourite platform stories was of the old boy who appeared at the polls for the first time in fif-teen years, when the Liberals had indicated sympathy for the suf-fragettes. Queried as to what had brought him out, he replied: "You bet I came out today to vote against givin' these fool women a vote; what's the good of givin' them a vote? They wouldn't use it!"

Petitions showered on the new Manitoba Legislature. Premier Norris had backtracked on his commitment to women's suffrage, say-ing that he would not introduce a bill unless its need was popularly indicated. Forty thousand signatures were his answer. One petition alone had 4,250 names gathered by ninety-four-year-old Mrs. Amelia Burritt of Sturgeon Creek.

All the writing, speaking and dreary footwork of the suffragettes finally paid off on January 27th, 1916, when the Bill for the Enfranchisement of Women was passed unanimously: "The Bill is reported without amendment, Mr. Speaker. God Save the King." The women of Manitoba could at last vote in provincial elections.

The uproar of cheers and desk-thumping was deafening. Everyone in the Chamber broke into a lusty singing of *O Canada*, followed by the rollicking strains of *For They Are Jolly Good Fellows* from the women in the galleries. Members leapt to their feet and sang it back to the ladies with equal "verve and melody," the press reported. The oldest surviving member of the House said he had never seen anything like it.

What Nellie had called "a bonny fight, a knockdown drag-out fight, uniting the women of Manitoba in a great cause" had been resolved in victory, but the brave little general had not been able to be present. A congratulatory telegram was sent from the House, "from the women voters of Manitoba to Mrs. McClung for the great service she has rendered her cause in Manitoba."

Members vied for the Speaker's eye. Everyone wanted to get into the act on this historic occasion. There were allusions to the Magna Carta, to the Garden of Eden, to the lustre which women would add to the House. There were "numerous humorous sallies, droll and pointed anecdotes which kept the house and Galleries in roars of laughter," the press tells us.

Later that year the *Times* of Fairmont, West Virginia, reported: "If all the women of Canada are like Nellie McClung, who addressed a crowded house at the circuit courtroom last evening, then there can be small wonder that women in Canada are allowed to vote... she gave an address teeming with brilliant thought and interesting con- clusions... and packed with humour."

After the bill for enfranchisement of women received royal assent the first week in February, a banquet was given at the Royal Alexandra Hotel under the auspices of the Political Equality League. Included in the gathering were members of the Legislature and the heads of many important organizations in the province. Seated at the head table, among the dignitaries, was old Mrs. Amelia Burritt, of petition fame. "I'd like to be able to vote on prohibition," she said, "for I've fought hard for it. However I am confident this reform will not be long delayed."

Nineteen speeches were delivered, along with toasts and replies to them. Presumably the toasts were drunk in Adam's Ale. Dr. Mary Crawford proposed the toast to the Premier – "the first minister of the first province to grant women's suffrage in Canada." In his reply, the Premier spoke of a casual encounter in the States – a chap who was astonished to hear about the suffrage bill. Not knowing Premier Norris's identity, the "Yankee"

WCTU Temperance Pledge

burst out, "What sort of a man must you have at the head of the government? He must be a henpecked husband anyway."

The Premier went on to say: "If the women of the civilized countries had enjoyed the franchise ten years ago, then Mr. Kaiser Bill of Germany would not be doing what he is today, for he would have had the privilege of being counseled and influenced by women as well as men. We hope the war will come soon to an end, but we must express our admiration of what the ladies of the Dominion are doing in this great crisis."

Almost as a corollary to the suffrage bill, the Manitoba Temperance Act (June, 1916) was passed. Liquor could henceforth be sold in the province only by druggists on a doctor's prescription. A period began which was referred to by many Manitobans as the "long drought." But it was a period welcomed by the WCTU, and by many pharmacists, who grew strangely affluent.

Sharing newspaper space with "Suffrage Husbands Praise Their Wives. Testify in public that Women who want to Vote make Good Life-Partners," were such items as: "Plan Underway to Recruit the 184th," "President Wilson on Side of Justice. Declares Liberty and Honour of the United States more Important than Peace," and "Late List of Wounded Canadian Officers and Where Being Cared For."

Jubilation was tempered with trepidation. Jack, the McClungs' first-born, had gone marching off to war. Nellie had written in her diary December 4th, 1915: "Strange fate surely for a boy who has never had a gun in his hands, whose ways are gentle and full of peace; who loves his fellow men, pities their sorrows, and would

Edith Rogers

gladly help them to solve their problems. What have I done to you, in letting you go into this inferno of war? And how could I hold you back without breaking your heart?"

Even in the area of female suffrage, jubilation was short-lived. Had Nellie McClung stayed in Manitoba, the political story might have been different. Who can say? But the women in the Political Equality League, exhausted by their long struggle, assumed that once women had the vote, the natural female good house-keeping spirit would take over. The political house would be set in order and reforms would follow as night does day. But in fact the League disbanded in 1917, leaderless. Women's clubs thought it more trendy to go in for the intensive study of Renaissance art or early Greek drama than the "unladylike" probing of the political process.

The first woman elected to the Manitoba Legislature was Edith Rogers in 1920. Ontario sent the first woman, Agnes McPhail, to the federal House in 1921. The only woman from Manitoba to sit in the House of Commons was Edith Rogers' daughter, Margaret Konantz, elected in 1963.

Oh Brave New World!

But the ice had been broken, and now other provinces were following Manitoba's lead: Alberta declared women eligible to vote provincially in April, 1916. The Wartime Elections Act, 1917, allowed women a toe in the federal door of enfranchisement. Because of the difficulty of obtaining votes from service personnel in the trenches of France, the Act declared that, "such of their kin at home who can best be said to be likely to vote in such a way as they themselves would do upon our shores" would be permitted to cast a ballot. There was no mention of the rights of women: women's votes could be cast only on behalf of men.

The Minister of Trade and Commerce made it clear that this was a special case in the special circumstances of war. Women could vote who were giving the service and making the sacrifice "which comes from heart strings wrung, which looks out of tear-bedimmed eyes, which comes from sleepless nights and anxious days, which comes from the part of flesh and blood that is far from them and which is exposed to constant danger... This is the distinguishing line upon which we base this Franchise Bill."

But in the final year of the war, all women were at last granted the right to vote federally. Borden, in moving the Bill, spoke of "the wonderful and conspicuous sacrifice which women have rendered to the national cause in the war." Yet this was not the main reason for enfranchisement. "Apart from all of these, I conceive that women are entitled to the franchise on their merits, and it is upon this basis that this Bill is presented to Parliament to its consideration."

In 1918, after the Bill had been passed, Nellie was called to the Dominion War Conference in Ottawa by Sir Robert Borden. Borden now headed a Union government – a rather uneasy alliance of Conservatives and some Liberals – which had brought in conscription in 1917. The conference was called to discuss the national registration of women, food conservation, child welfare and national health policies.

The Ottawa press reported that "Mrs. McClung delivered an inspiring and illuminated address at the luncheon of delegates today. She said that the elimination of alcoholic beverages on an Empire prohibition basis is one of the certain reforms that will evolve from the world-wide conflict." Nellie never stopped dreaming the impossible dream.

War and politics had not kept Nell from writing. Two of her books had been published in war-time. *In Times Like These* (1915) and *The Next of Kin* (1917) were collections of essays and sketches containing a great deal of sound philosophizing.

Three Times and Out, which was published in 1918, was the story "as told by Private Simmons to Nellie McClung" of an escaped prisoner of war. With three new books to her credit, and with two of her dearest goals realized – prohibition and the enfranchisement of women – Nellie McClung could be well pleased with her efforts. But there were still new doors to open.

Chapter 9
The Stream Runs Fast

In 1921, at the age of forty-eight, Nellie McClung was elected as a Liberal member to the Alberta Legislature. Fittingly enough, it meant sitting as a member of the opposition: the Liberal government had been badly trounced by the United Farmers of Alberta, who now formed the government.

True to her convictions, Nellie supported legislation, no matter which party introduced it, for old age pensions, for mothers' allowances, for amendments to the Dower Act, for establishing better conditions in factories, for a minimum wage, prohibition, birth control and more liberal divorce. ("Why are pencils equipped with erasers? Everyone makes mistakes.") Alberta had the first Act in the British Empire authorizing the sterilization of the unfit. It was the first province to have public health nurses, municipal hospitals, and free dental and medical care for schoolchildren.

It was once said that Nellie McClung would be able to pick out the Alberta women when she got to Heaven: they would be huddled in little groups, notebooks in hand, composing resolutions – advocating the presence of more rural children in the Heavenly Choir, perhaps.

Women were taking their places in the political arena, but the church was slow to use their services. Nellie ironically remarked that "the women may lift the mortgages or build churches or any other light work, but the really heavy work of the church, such as moving resolutions in the general conferences... must be done by strong hardy men." The "strong hardy men" called her bluff on this one and sent Nellie as the only woman among twelve Methodist delegates to the Ecumenical Conference in London, England.

To her despair, she discovered that even at this Christian gathering there was race prejudice and intolerance. But although she was disappointed with the conference, Nellie met many warm, friendly people in the informal gatherings that took place.

Never one to waste an opportunity, she stayed in London an extra month and loved every minute of it. She visited France too and made a pilgrimage to the War Cemeteries with their acres of white crosses.

That same year, 1921, *Purple Springs* was published. This is a romanticized version of her own battle for women's suffrage. The fictional form gave her the liberty to omit unpleasant things and finish with a happy ending.

At a Canadian Authors' Association meeting, Nellie expressed her belief that: "It is the writer's place to bring romance to people, to turn the commonplace into the adventurous and the amusing, to bring out the pathos in a situation... Words are our tools and must be kept bright... I refuse to be carried through the sewers of life just for the ride... I write if I have something to say that will amuse, entertain, instruct, inform, comfort or guide the reader."

When Christmas Crossed "The Peace," a short novel, came out in 1923. That year Wes was again transferred, and the McClungs moved to Calgary. This meant that Nellie led a bisected life. When the provincial House was in session, she stayed in Edmonton during the week and went home to Calgary on weekends. Without her family in Edmonton, she used any free time to study. She was busy with research for her next novel, the story of a young Finnish girl. All the resources of the provincial library were available to her and she read everything she could lay her hands on about Finland and the Finnish people. Like Emily Dickinson, Nellie always asked herself, "Have I said it true?"

Nellie

The fact that Finnish women had the vote and sat in parliament long before women were granted those rights in any other country, plus the fact that she had a Finnish girl working for her, inspired Nellie to write *Painted Fires* (1925), considered by many to be her best novel.

The theme of the book is that "we cannot warm ourselves at painted fires." The heroine reaches a desperately low point and questions the authenticity of God himself: "and God, her God, who had seemed so close and dear and loving to her, was he just a painted fire, like the other, cold and dead, and mocking, when she came to him crying and shivering, bitterly alone, and afraid?"

The young Finnish heroine, Helmi (in spite of her adventures in a dope den, a prison, a rescue home for "fallen" girls where mother-hood is regarded as a punishment for sin, a rough mining camp, and a police court), remains almost virginally good, charming all about her with her vivid personality.

Nellie lacks Dickens' bravura and rich depth of character, but it is quite apparent that he is her model. Dickensian coincidences abound. She, like Dickens, uses long, well-written descriptive pas-sages. She shares with Dickens the ability to highlight those details which will vividly convey the setting of her stories, as in this descrip-tion of a little country train station, with its stove "either fireless or red hot... torn posters showing palatial white steamers plowing green seas carrying pleasure-seeking Canadians to tropical lands... a notice re a bull pup answering to the name of 'Buster'... a dance and raffle by St. Faith's Ladies Aid, cordial invitation to all... John Fernwaldt's announcement of his ability to mend shoes, Old Country methods and moderate prices – try me once."

Like Dickens, Nellie works her crusades into her novels too. Helmi would like to build her own house, but realizes that being a girl makes it impossible. Later she reflects, "here she was, working all day long for twenty-five dollars a month, while the poorest man in the mines had four dollars a day and only worked eight hours. It sure was the limit!"

Nellie's loathing of war is conveyed in a scene where an old vet-eran speaks: "Shook me up quite a lot the day I lost my leg... Later there was great explanations and beg-your-pardons and excuses and after-you-sirs, but no legs handed back."

The book went through many editions, was translated into Finnish, and had an excellent reception in Finland. Nellie elected to receive her royalties for the sales there in the form of two beautiful oil paintings. In addition, the Finnish government sent her a book about Finland "with the best wishes of all Helmi's countrymen."

Nellie was soon to have more time for her writing. A provincial referendum in 1924 ended the prohibition which had existed since 1916 in Alberta. But Nellie was still working to bring it back. Before the provincial election in 1926, some hotelkeepers came to her secretly and promised they would vote for her in a body if she would lay off her anti-liquor propaganda. But our longtime WCTU-er stood firm. Perhaps because of this, she was defeated by sixty votes. This came as a bitter blow to her pride. Nellie always liked to be a winner.

But she was not going to mope. After she heard the results, she set off at once on "a perfect debauch of cooking... the old stone sugar crock with the cracked and handleless cup in it seemed glad to see me... I do not think I could have endured it that day if my cooking had gone wrong, but nothing failed me and no woman can turn out an ovenfull of good flaky pies... and not find peace for her troubled soul."

Now she threw herself with redoubled vigour into her writing. She churned out columns, homilies, and a short story a week.

The first book Nellie published after her political defeat was a collection of short stories and essays, reprinted from various periodicals, called *All We Like Sheep*, which appeared in 1926. The title essay is an amusing tale of Nellie's venture into sheep-raising.

Nellie bought the sheep with the assurance that this was a most prolific group and she would have a prodigious number of spring lambs for sale. But Nellie was suspicious from the start: as the ewes "sidled past they gave me a sort of Mona Lisa smirk... so smug, so prim... such an insufferable time-will-tell look that I felt sure they were pulling off a joke." She found out what the 'joke' was when lambing time came round. There was "nothing to prove that they had lived, except in a few cases, anything but blameless lives... Only a few of them had any domestic tendencies... but as raising stock they were hard to beat."

All her friends found the project highly amusing. One wag sent her a Christmas card picturing an old lady knitting with sheep placidly grazing nearby, accompanied by this verse:

In nineteen hundred and fifty-two
These may be them, this may be you,
If they escape the wolves and ticks,
And you keep out of politics.

Nellie McClung's fiction tends to rework a few basic plot-lines. Again and again in her stories the pursuit of unbridled pleasure brings its own damnation, or else the sinner suffers and then repents. The characters too are somewhat stereotyped. "City slickers" are usually money-grubbing and selfish, whereas country folk are warm, loving, and neighbourly.

There are no open endings in McClung stories. All the strings are pulled neatly together and there are nothing but blue skies from then on. Sales indicated that there were plenty of people who liked things this way.

Nellie L. McClung. 1914.

Chapter 10
Women Become Persons

In addition to her writing, Nellie had "meetings to be attended, letters written, bills paid, coal to order, meals to cook, tag-days, receptions, delegations, resolutions, amendments, saving clauses, committees, dressmakers... and above all earth's clamour, cutting through it, insistent, commanding, imperative, not to be denied or ignored comes the ring of the telephone."

There were constant calls on her to speak at Young People's Clubs, Literary Clubs, Social Service groups and so on. Under the aegis of the American National Suffrage Association, she spoke in more than half the states of the Union.

Women had achieved some recognition, but there was still a long way to go. An advertisement for the 1926 *Encyclopedia Britannica* touted an article on "Woman – Yesterday and Today." "Despite the restriction of ancient customs, laws and privileges, woman has at last established her rightful claim to equal privileges with man. Her manifold activities and achievements have amazed the world. Her wisdom, charm and genius have won inevitable recognition."

But there was evidence to the contrary, as the famous Persons Case proved.

Edmonton had the first woman magistrate in Canada – Emily Murphy (who wrote under the name Janey Canuck). But Emily Murphy was faced with prejudice – and with the vagaries of the law.

Back in 1876 an Englishwoman had had the temerity to vote, had been arrested for her misdemeanor, and the judge had ruled that "Women are persons in matters of pain and penalties, but are not persons in matters of rights and privileges." This ruling was still in effect.

In 1917, a defense lawyer, testy at the stiff sentence Emily Murphy had given his client, used this ruling to challenge her authority to hand down a judicial decision. The Alberta Supreme Court upheld her authority, but the matter rankled in Emily's soul. If women were not "persons," some doors were still closed to them. For example, there were no women in the Canadian Senate: section 24 of the British North America Act read that "the Governor-

General shall from time to time in the Queen's name summon qualified persons to the Senate." There was that word again: persons.

From 1919 to 1922, many groups (including the Federated
Women's Institutes, the National Council of Women and the
Montreal Women's Club) all sparked by Emily Murphy, pressured
the Prime Minister to appoint a woman to the Senate. By August,
1927 the women were exasperated by the unconcern and inaction of
five administrations – Borden's, Meighen's, King's, Meighen's and
King's again. A group of five women including Emily Murphy and
Nellie McClung formally petitioned Prime Minister Mackenzie King
for an interpretation of the Act. "Does the word Persons in Section
24 of the British North America Act, 1867, include female persons?"

*Prime Minister King honour-
ing Emily Murphy, Henrietta
Muir Edwards, Louise
McKinney, Irene Parlby (and
at right) Nellie McClung*

Women Become Persons

As in A.A.Milne's well-known verse "the king asked the queen and the queen asked the dairymaid...," the Prime Minister referred it to the Minister of Justice, who in turn referred it to the Supreme Court of Canada. The petition snailed through all the bureaucratic In and Out baskets until, in April of 1928, the Supreme Court decided that women were most definitely not persons within the meaning of the Act.

The Valiant Five did not give up: in July 1929 they took their case to the Privy Council in London, England, at that time the final Court of Appeal for Canadians. (It was not until 1949 that the Supreme Court of Canada became the final court of appeal.)

That august body argued for four days whether women could legally be considered persons. Then they went home and cogitated quietly for three months. Finally, on October 18th, 1929 newspapers all over the British Empire headlined, "Privy Council Declares that Women are Persons." It came as a nasty shock to most women, who had gone along for years under the happy misapprehension that they were already persons.

Whether Mackenzie King's "spirits" advised him or whether he was just plain vindictive, he did not do the decent thing and appoint Emily Murphy to the Senate. He appointed Cairine Wilson as the first woman – and that not until 1930. In 1931, when an Edmonton senator died, the logical choice would again have been Judge Murphy; but R.B. Bennett, then the Prime Minister, said he was "morally obligated" to replace a Roman Catholic by another of the same faith.

In 1938 the Business and Professional Women of Canada placed a memorial plaque in the foyer of the Senate Chamber in Ottawa honouring the Valiant Five: Emily Murphy, Nellie McClung, Henrietta Edwards, author of *Laws Relating to Women*, Louise McKinney, the first woman to sit in a Legislature in the British Empire, and Irene Parlby who for fourteen years was a member of the Alberta Cabinet. These women made it possible for women in Canada to be appointed to the Senate.

Chapter 11
Depression and War

The long hot summer of 1929 ended and the ten lost years of the Great Depression began. Prairie wheat sold for an all-time low of 38c a bushel. People returned to primitive barter methods of payment. "Bennett Buggies" – cars pulled by horses – were routinely seen on the prairies since people had no money for gas or repairs. Life there was particularly hard: the years of the Depression coincided with one of the worst droughts the prairies had ever known.

Nellie chided the government for not rushing in with more employment relief projects, such as house – and road – building and water conservation. In 1935, Albertans as a whole expressed their dissatisfaction with the existing government by electing William Aberhart as Premier. Aberhart, an evangelical radio preacher, was the leader of the newly-formed Social Credit Party. He was greatly influenced by the theories expressed by Major C.H. Douglas in his book, *Social Credit*.

Aberhart blamed the Depression on "eastern" financial interests and international bankers. He promised a cash dividend of $25 a month to every Albertan resident. With his Bible in one hand and his "funny money" in the other, Bill Aberhart looked pretty attractive to the depressed, Depression-weary people. His Social Credit government was to remain in power for over thirty years.

The Depression years were hard, but they were not unproductive ones for Nellie. She published two more volumes of short stories in 1930 and 1931, *Be Good to Yourself* and *Flowers for the Living*.

In 1935, Wes retired and the McClungs moved to Gordonhead near Victoria. They hung one of the treasured Finnish oil paintings over the

Bennett Buggy

Unemployed march at Calgary, 1935

fireplace in the dark green, shingled bungalow on Lantern Lane. Retirement, for Nellie, meant that she could devote more time to her writing.

She had already started work on her autobiography. The first volume was published in 1935 under the title *Clearing in the West*. The second volume, *The Stream Runs Fast*, did not appear for another ten years. These two well-written books contain a remarkable record of the first half of the century in western Canada.

Nellie found that the freedom to write uninterruptedly did not produce the expected results right away: "for two terrible days I sat looking at the paper with my mind as dry as a covered bridge." Once she began to put pen to paper, however, the flow of words returned.

Nellie McClung's approach to autobiography was to retain the privacy of her intimate relationships, and relate in detail her public life and the society and personalities of her time.

"I had seen the beginning of so many things: women's struggle for political equality, the rise of women's clubs, the heroic struggle to eliminate the liquor traffic and its disastrous sequel... I wanted to put into words what I knew of those women who had been too busy making history to write it.

"I have seen my country emerge from obscurity into one of the truly great nations of the world... People must know the past

Premier William Aberhart, leader of the newly-formed Social Credit Party

to understand the present and to face the future."

Nellie's writing had the same mixture of righteousness and fervour that was found in her life. It is said in animal husbandry that verve and spirit come from the sire and stamina from the dam. So it was with Nellie McClung. From her Irish father she inherited wit, vivacity, and love of poetry and music; from her Scottish mother she acquired Presbyterian strength, courage, rectitude and compassion. ("Mother always took to homely people and bitter medicine.") This combination made for an interesting personality, and although at times it gave her writing the flavour of the Sunday School hymn, it was always lightened by a spirit of fun and a warm and human loving kindness. She managed to keep her hand on her heart even when she had her tongue in her cheek.

During these prolific writing years, Nellie remained active in public affairs. In 1936 she was appointed as the first woman member of the new Canadian Broadcasting Corporation's Board of Governors, a position she held for six years.

Nellie had great expectations of the CBC. She told the Women's Canadian Club in Winnipeg in 1937 that she had high hopes for the improvement in the quality of life in Canada now that good music, travel talks, book reviews and so on were available in the home.

Radio, she was sure, would foster new understanding between the industrial east and the agricultural west. In 1937, sixty percent of the territory of Canada was reached by the airwaves of the CBC. Every radio owner paid an annual license fee of two dollars which, she said proudly, was the lowest of any country in the world which imposed a radio tax.

"I would rather be a member of the Board of Governors of the CBC than be a member of the Board of Governors of the largest university in the country," she concluded, "because it has the greatest student body, the lowest fees and the easiest entrance exams."

Sometimes Nellie wondered if she was becoming too old to attend to public duties. When, in July of 1938, she was invited by the federal Department of Agriculture to be the keynote speaker at the Silver Jubilee of the Women's Institute to be held in Nova Scotia, she accused herself of "middle-aged vanity" in accepting. She wondered, "Why am I tearing myself to pieces pretending I am as good as ever?" But, at sixty-four, she was indeed "as good as ever." The Department had lured her with the promise of a visit round the whole peninsula. She simply couldn't refuse.

While still in Nova Scotia, she was electrified to learn that the Prime Minister had appointed her as one of the Canadian delegates to the League of Nations' Nineteenth Assembly in Geneva in September.

The League, predecessor to the United Nations, had been created in 1920 by the Treaty of Versailles. That agreement, the peace treaty after World War 1, was conceived as a move to prevent further wars. But the Allies demanded reparations from Germany which the Germans (and even some Allies) considered "grotesque" in size, and the Versailles Treaty became, not a solution, but the cause of further friction. The League of Nations was conceived in the same spirit as the Treaty, but the fact that neither the United States (which had not ratified the treaty) nor the defeated powers of the First World War were represented in the League weakened its effectiveness from the start.

While she was in Switzerland before the League assembled, Nellie seized the opportunity to attend a meeting of the Oxford Group, an evangelical Christian movement. She sent press reports back to Canada.

She felt that the times were sadly out of joint. "*Temperance*" and "*prohibition*" were still words which did not "fire the heather." On the contrary, more people were drinking than ever before. "We need a united forward movement and I believe the Oxford Groups are giving it. The severest criticism of their members is that

First CBC Board of Governors

they live at good hotels, dress for dinner and travel first class... There is a tendency in our minds to associate holy living with poverty, and people, as a rule, like to have religion remain obscure and humble, modest, unobtrusive and slightly apologetic."

Her own faith was vigorous and positive. "Doctrinal discussions have a moldy taste and are dusty to the palate." But, "when I get to Heaven I will have a few questions. No doubt there will be certain days set apart when even a private member can interrogate the government – such as – How is it that a just God has allowed the sins of the fathers to be visited on the children?"

Biblical language had great appeal for Nellie: "I love the Bible for its stately music and the elegance of its diction and the words of Christ have the power to set all the bells in my heart ringing."

Nellie had no patience with the "simpering, tea-drinking bazaar-opening curates, pallid and dandruffy with decayed teeth." "God demands our love," she declared, "not just our amiability. Amiability never gets anyone in wrong but love may and often does kill... The gardener who loves flowers must destroy the weeds." She admired the "modern preacher who comes boldly into public life." She did not suffer fools gladly.

At the Nineteenth Assembly in Geneva, Nellie was made a member of the Fifth Committee of the League of Nations, which dealt with social legislation, refugees, narcotics, nutrition, housing and labour conditions. She felt that as a research bureau and clearing house of ideas, the League was reasonably successful, but as a police court for the community of nations, it was failing miserably: in 1931, Japan had invaded China, and the League had done nothing.

Nellie believed that "Peace is not a pale negative, a state of doing nothing. Peace has to be worked for, and bought at great price. Peace may even mean a sacrifice of someone's dignity and the giving up of someone's dearest prejudices."

The League of Nations seemed to her like a well-built house, with all the wiring carefully and efficiently installed, in which no one had turned on the power. At the Oxford Group meeting, by contrast, she had felt the power of God sparking along the lines.

In the last week of September, 1938, all the League of Nations delegates heard Adolf Hitler (the man Mackenzie King in 1937 had called "too simple to be dangerous") screaming on the radio that he would march on Czechoslovakia on October 1st. The Hon. Ernest Lapointe, leader of the Canadian delegation, was recalled home. His parting remark was: "There will not be war, I think, for at least a year. But we must be ready for anything. Hitler means business!"

Hitler did indeed mean business. In September, 1939, Canada, for the first time, declared war as a separate nation. The 1931 Statute of Westminster had ended control of Canada's affairs from Britain. Canada, a Dominion which stretched *a mari usque ad mare*, had become a voluntary partner in the British Commonwealth of Nations. Nellie McClung, who had been born only six years after Confederation, now witnessed her country emerging as an independent nation.

The McClung Family

Chapter 12
Leaves from Lantern Lane

Throughout Wes's retirement years, Nellie's compulsion to write continued. Two volumes of collected essays, *Leaves from Lantern Lane* (1936) and *More Leaves From Lantern Lane* (1937), contain some of her best writing.

All her work was well received. At least five of her books sold 25,000 copies each. Her publisher estimated that her income from her books was close to $60,000.

Nellie unquestionably had the good newspaper columnist's ability to take a slight subject, treat it with dignity and humour, and ennoble it with thoughtful comment.

She laughingly complained: "I have a fatal gift for starting monologues. If there is a vein of idle ore anywhere in my vicinity, I will be sure as fate to tap it with some innocent word." This was one of the secrets of her strongest writing which, with maturity, had become better and better. Her early fiction, understandably, did not measure up in quality to her later essays and autobiography. Not only did she have a taperecorder mind, she was genuinely interested in, and sympathetic to, the sorrows, joys and hopes of everyone with whom she came in contact.

As was the way with Vancouver Island residents, the McClungs became passionate gardeners. When Wes wasn't golfing – the family claimed he hunted lost balls with a flashlight, he got up so early – he was gardening. He was still physically fit and fine-looking with a clear ruddy complexion, his auburn hair just sprinkled with grey. He retained the zest of a boy, and enjoyed his food with a boy's relish. A great deal of that food the family grew themselves.

A friend for whom Wes had done a favour once remarked that he hoped Wes would get his crown in Heaven. Wes replied: "No, I don't want a crown, all I want is a good spade and a piece of ground – and a river nearby."

The house was always blooming with bouquets gathered from the McClung garden. Lavender flowers could often be seen drying, in preparation for making little scented bags for friends. Nellie was now getting fan mail from all over Canada asking for her advice on both marital and gardening problems.

Her home and garden were delights to her. She wrote about the threat of thrips, about sweet peas, "leggy and decrepit and full of rickets," and about the local wildlife, "that spring robin I thought I saw, which turned out to be a sparrow wearing his red flannels."

Nellie's creative mind was always at work no matter what her hands were doing. She could see "books in the running brooks, sermons in stones..." At the drop of a hat – or a gardening hoe – she could philosophize on gulls, quails, growing onions, or bees:

"Bees... big stumbling fellows in black velvet and gold... there is something uncanny about bees with their perfect organization, their distribution of work and wages, their orderly marketing and effective way of regulating the population, and their dealing with unemployment. It is impossible to feel superior and wise in the presence of a bee!"

She applied her wit to anything, from wealthy widows: "A widow with money is a shining mark for a mining shark," to tardy trains – the prairie train "did not run by the clock and sometimes it ignored the calendar" – and to money acquired without labour:

Nellie and grandchild

The banker calls it interest and winks the other eye
The merchant calls it profit and heaves a joyful sigh
The landlord calls it rentals and he puts it in his bag
The good old honest burglar – he just calls it swag.

For the Hyena in Petticoats who had said, "Never retreat, never explain, never apologize. Get the thing done and let them howl," these were gentle, mellowed years.

A typically domestic scene – tomatoes ripening on the window sill, Wes sitting on the blue rocking chair beside the old wood stove, with the black cat, King Faruk, tinkling the bells on his leather collar as he rubbed against Wes's legs – would be completed by Nellie sitting at her desk writing, or else struggling over some difficult clue in a crossword puzzle.

"My grandchildren and great-grandchildren will get no socks from me, done by my own frail and trembling old fingers. Not a sock. On the contrary I will expect them to tell me what half an em is, and what is the Portuguese word for bread."

Some people had always claimed that the terms "suffragette" and "happy marriage" were mutually exclusive. But they were wrong. In 1946, the McClungs celebrated their fiftieth wedding anniversary surrounded by their family.

Nellie and Wes with family, at their 50th wedding anniversary.

Leaves from Lantern Lane

The independent spirit who, before she met Wes, maintained that "marriage seems like the end of all ambition, hope and aspiration," now merrily told the press: "The day I married Wes I did the best day's work I have ever done."

She pointed out that after she had deferred to his judgment on fountain-pen merits that long-ago day in the Manitou drugstore, "he had no chance to escape."

The family attended morning service at St. Aidan's United Church on Mount Tolmie and came home to a family dinner at Lantern Lane. In the afternoon the anniversary couple held court, greeting old friends in their hillside garden.

Nellie told the press: "I am sure through husband and wife developing their own individuality without impinging on each other, happiness is assured."

Their love had remained steadfast through the years – they still continued to laugh at each other's jokes.

Eventually, arthritis and heart problems forced Nellie to slacken her pace. She did no more writing, but she continued her private acts of kindness and never lost her interest in people.

Nor did she ever lose her childlike sense of wonder and anticipation, or her delight in simple things. She always expected something really exciting to appear around the next bend in the road. Children recognized this quality in her, and also felt a heady sense of their own importance and worth when they were talking to her.

Education of the young was always dear to Nellie: "If I were young again I would spend my life as a teacher of young children, doing all in my power to give them a vision of the dignity and glory of being builders and planters, makers and menders."

When a Nellie McClung Collegiate in Manitou was opened in 1964, her daughter, Florence Atkinson, said: "I can't think of a more fitting tribute to my mother, or one she would have preferred, to having a school named after her."

Nellie's ideals had always been high, and in spite of setbacks and some disillusionment, her basic faith in humanity never faltered. Although her belief that women would use the vote to make the world a better, cleaner place, that the "sound of the political carpet beater would be heard in the land," had never really been fulfilled, Nellie could still say: "I believe in the ultimate end of humanity, and I believe in the human race, in spite of its shortcomings, as the expression of divinity upon earth, and leading onward and upward to something brighter and better. I believe that there is nothing too good to be true."

Nellie McClung died on September 1st, 1951, gallantly, as she had lived.

Leaves from Lantern Lane

Chapter 13
Epilogue

The one hundredth anniversary of Nellie McClung's birth was celebrated in a number of ways. One honour was the issuing of a commemorative Nellie McClung stamp, which was released in 1973. It was an honour marred for some by the unattractive way Nellie was portrayed, however: she was depicted as the stereotype of a thin-lipped, repressive, intractable temperance worker, bearing little resemblance to the warm, outgoing, vivacious woman with soft, dark hair and glinting cinnamon-brown eyes who was adored by thousands as "Our Nell."

During the ceremony at the Winnipeg Inn in August, 1973, announcing the issue of the stamp, her son, Mark, said, "Mother was a radical Christian – a free thinker. She wanted to be a clergyman but women couldn't then be ordained."

Mark McClung, a Rhodes Scholar from Alberta in 1935, continued his mother's work: he headed the research team of the Royal Commission on the Status of Women which reported in 1973. It had met over a period of nearly four years, studying and holding public hearings.

The Commission was to recommend what steps the federal government might take to ensure for women equal opportunities with men in every aspect of Canadian society: political rights, role in the Canadian labour force, better use of skills, federal labour laws in relation to women, employment and promotion of women in the federal service, federal taxation, marriage and divorce, position of women under criminal law, immigration and citizenship laws.

It was not an easy task, and, in spite of the inroads made by women such as Nellie McClung, there was still a long way to go. An editorial in the Ottawa *Journal*, October 3rd, 1968, made the comment: "A dozen Royal Commissions probably wouldn't be enough to illustrate all the dark corners of male prejudice. There is something ingrained in our culture that has made the struggle of women for full equality under the law slow and unfinished business. Men, it seems, like it that way."

After the Commission had made its report, an Advisory Council on the Status of Women, consisting of thirty hard-working members, was formed. Gradually, most of the Commission's 167 recommendations have been adopted.

When women in the 1970s were still fighting for equal rights, it seemed incredible that the ball had started to roll as long ago as the late eighteenth century, with the appearance of Mary Wollstonecraft's famous *Vindication of the Rights of Women.* In her time, Mary Wollstonecraft was hated because she asserted women's right to social and economic independence. Two hundred years later, in 1974, women accounted for 34% of Canada's labour force, but a survey indicated that only 4% of managerial positions were held by women. How much had changed?

The fight continued with increasing success. There has been a continuous upsurge of interest in the status of women, and women's studies has become well established as a legitimate subject in higher education. Nellie McClung and her peers are becoming increasingly revered for the part they played in this progress.

As Martha Hynna, of the Canadian delegation to the United Nations Commission on the Status of Women for International Women's Year, 1975 said:

> "In the long run, all the hassles of women's groups will have been well worth the effort if the barriers of human prejudice can be worn away and everyone can share equally in the responsibilities of our society."

In recent years women have achieved such prominent political positions as Speaker of the House of Commons, Justices of the Supreme Court of Canada, Lieutenant-Governor of the Province of Ontario, president of the Liberal Party of Canada, and Governor-General of Canada.

A clause guaranteeing equal rights and freedoms to men and women was also included as part of Canada's Constitution in the 1982 Charter of Rights and Freedoms, and, thanks to the lobbying efforts of many women and women's rights organizations, this clause cannot be overruled by an act of the federal or provincial governments (as some other clauses in the Charter can be).

Much has changed for women since Nellie McClung's day, but many reforms in law and society must still be made. If Nellie McClung were alive today, she would surely still be on the ramparts, talking, persuading, arguing and fighting for a better world. Indeed, her spirit lives on in the thoughts and deeds of countless men and women who have been inspired by her example to continue the struggle in which she played so great a role.

Further Reading

Nellie McClung's sixteen published books are:

Sowing Seeds in Danny. Toronto: William Briggs, 1908.
The Second Chance. Toronto: William Briggs, 1910.
The Black Creek Stopping House. Toronto: William Briggs, 1912.
In Times Like These. Toronto: McLeod & Allen, 1915. (Re-issued in 1972 by University of Toronto Press.)
The Next of Kin. Toronto: Thomas Allen and Son, 1917.
Three Times and Out. Toronto: Thomas Allen and Son, 1918.
Purple Springs. Toronto: Thomas Allen and Son, 1921.
When Christmas Crossed "The Peace." Toronto: Thomas Allen and Son , 1923.
Painted Fires. Toronto: Thomas Allen and Son, 1925.
All We Like Sheep. Toronto: Thomas Allen and Son, 1926.
Be Good To Yourself. Toronto: Thomas Allen and Son, 1930.
Flowers for the Living. Toronto: Thomas Allen and Son, 1931.
Clearing in the West. Toronto: Thomas Allen and Son, 1935

(Autobiography)
    Firing the Heather: The Life and Times of Nellie McClung, Mary Hallet and Marilyn Davis. Calgary: Fifth House, 1993.
Leaves from Lantern Lane. Toronto: Thomas Allen and Son, 1936.
More Leaves from Lantern Lane. Toronto: Thomas Allen and Son, 1937.
The Stream Runs Fast. Toronto: Thomas Allen and Son, 1945. (Autobiography)

Other Books of Interest
The Woman Suffrage Movement in Canada. Catherine, Lyle, Cleverdon. Toronto: University of Toronto Press, 1950.
Manitoba: A History. W.L. Morton, W.L., Toronto: University of Toronto Press, 1967.
Recalled to Life. M.J.G., McMullen, Winnipeg, Manitoba Travel and Convention Association, 1966

Credits

The publisher wishes to express its gratitude to the following who have given permission to use copyrighted illustrations in this book:

The author wishes to thank the following for their help: the Main Branch of the Winnipeg Public Library; University of Manitoba Library; Provincial Library at Manitoba; Provincial Archives of Manitoba; Manitoba Museum of Man and Nature; Catherine Lyle Cleverdon; Mrs. G.W.Burton; Penny Ham; Olive Irwin; Mary Konantz; Robert McKenzie; Mrs. Alex McPhail; Christine Moore; Charles Oke; Kay Rowe.

The publishers wish to express their gratitude to the following who have given permission to use copyrighted illustrations in this book:
Archives of Saskatchewan, 50, 51
British Columbia Archives, 19 (D-9034), 29 (B6791), 46 (HP39852), 57 (39855), 58 (39853)
Catherine Lyle Cleverton, 3
CBC, 54
Glenbow Archives, 5, 10, 13, 14, 15, 16, 18, 25, 26, 27
M.J.C. McMullen, 7
National Archives of Canada, 6, 12, 21, 32, 35, 37, 47, 60
The Winnipeg Free Press, 52

Index